D0120476

Aberdeenshire

3071979

23

Grimm's Fairy Tales

ABERDEENSHIRE LIBRARY & INFO SERV	
3071979	
Bertrams	02/04/2012
JS	£8.99

For Uncle Albert
S.P.

For Viggo
C.J.

ORCHARD BOOKS
338 Euston Road, London NW1 3BH
Orchard Books Australia
Level 17/207 Kent Street, Sydney, NSW 2000

This text was first published in the form of a gift collection called
The Sleeping Princess by Orchard Books in 2002

This edition first published in hardback in 2012
First paperback publication in 2013

ISBN 978 1 40830 841 7 (hardback)
ISBN 978 1 40830 842 4 (paperback)

Text © Saviour Pirotta 2002
Illustrations © Cecilia Johansson 2012

The rights of Saviour Pirotta to be identified as the author and
Cecilia Johansson to be identified as the illustrator of this work
have been asserted by them in accordance
with the Copyright, Designs and Patents Act, 1988.

A CIP catalogue record for this book is available
from the British Library.

1 3 5 7 9 10 8 6 4 2 (hardback)
1 3 5 7 9 10 8 6 4 2 (paperback)

Printed in China

Orchard Books is a division of Hachette Children's Books,
an Hachette UK company.
www.hachette.co.uk

Grimm's Fairy Tales

Rumpelstiltskin

Written by Saviour Pirotta

Illustrated by Cecilia Johansson

ORCHARD

Once there was a poor miller who had a beautiful daughter. He lived in a mill, on the edge of a wood where the king often went hunting.

"My daughter is so clever," he boasted to the king one day. "She can spin ordinary straw into gold."

The king loved gold more than anything.
"Send your daughter to my palace," he said
to the miller, "and we'll see if she can."

The next morning, when the miller's daughter arrived at the palace, the king showed her into a little chamber. He pointed to a big pile of straw and a spinning wheel.

"Spin this into gold by the morning,"
he said, "or I'll have you put to death."
Then the king locked and bolted the door.

The girl started to cry, for she had no way
of turning the straw to gold. Suddenly
the locked door opened and
a goblin came leaping in.

"What will you give me if I spin the straw
into gold for you?" he asked.
"My necklace," said the girl.

"Your necklace will do nicely,"
said the goblin.

He sat down at the wheel and started
spinning. In no time at all, the straw had been
spun into pure gold.

The goblin took the
girl's necklace and quickly
left the room.

At daybreak, the king unlocked the door.
When he saw the reels of gold, he clapped his
hands and servants brought in a pile
of straw twice as big as the first one.

"Spin that into gold or
you'll lose your head," he
said again. And he locked
and bolted the door once more.

The girl started weeping again. But no sooner had the sun set than the goblin appeared again.

"What will you give me if I spin your straw into gold once more?" he asked.

"I'll give you my ring," answered the girl.

"Your ring will do nicely," said the goblin. He took his place on the stool and the straw was soon a glittering heap of gold.

The king couldn't believe his eyes when he opened the door again at the crack of dawn.

He locked the girl in a room where there was a pile of straw THREE times the size of the first one.

At night, the goblin appeared and offered to help the girl again.

"But I have nothing left to give you," she said.

"Then promise to give me your first child when you have it," said the goblin.

The girl was so desperate, she promised the goblin her first baby.

The goblin sat at the stool. Once more the spinning wheel turned – *whirr, whirr, whirr* . . .

. . . and before sunrise the straw had been spun into shimmering gold.

In the morning, the king took the beautiful miller's daughter as his bride.

Time passed, and the new queen had a
baby. She was so happy, she forgot all about
the little goblin who had helped her.

But one night, the little man appeared,
grinning slyly from ear to ear.

"It's time you gave me what you promised,"
he said.

The young queen clasped the baby to her chest. "I will give you anything you ask for," she told the goblin, "but please don't take away my child."

"I am an honest man," said the goblin, "so I shall give you three days' grace."

"If you guess my name correctly, I shall let you keep the child."

The queen lay awake all night, trying to remember all the names she had ever heard.

Meanwhile, she sent out a messenger to track down all the unusual names he could find.

When the goblin arrived the next morning,
the queen started with the names she knew:
Alex, Peter, John . . . But the goblin just shook
his head at each and every one of them.

On the second day the queen repeated all the strange names she had read in the king's library: Loftus, Pimpernel, Fenugreek . . .

But once again the goblin shook his head.

On the third day, the messenger returned
with news. "Your Highness," he said, "I have
not been able to find a new name in two
days. But early this morning I came across
a little house with a log fire outside.

"Dancing on one foot was a curious goblin like the one you described. He was singing:

'Today I bake, tomorrow brew,
Merrily I dance and sing,
For the queen will never find out
My name is RUMPELSTILTSKIN.'"

When the queen heard the name, she started
singing and dancing herself.

As soon as the goblin arrived, she ushered him straight into her chamber. "Is your name Tom?" she said.

"I'm afraid that's not my name," answered the goblin.

"Then could it be Hamish?" asked the queen.

"I'm afraid it's not Hamish either," said the goblin.

"Well then," said the queen, "is it
RUMPELSTILTSKIN?"

The goblin was furious. "How did you find
that out?" he roared. He stamped his foot so
hard it went right through the floor.

He tried in vain to pull it out. In the end he
pulled so hard, he tore himself in two and died.

So the poor miller's daughter who had become queen, lived happily ever after with her king and her child.